How to Lose a Guy in 10 Dates

LACY WILLIAMS

Copyright © 2016 Lacy Williams

All rights reserved.

ISBN: 1-942505-08-6
ISBN-13: 978-1-942505-08-2

THE COWBOY FAIRYTALES SERIES

Once Upon a Cowboy
Cowboy Charming
The Toad Prince
The Beastly Princess
The Lost Princess

DEDICATION

For Levi.

PROLOGUE

Why had she ever agreed to this?

Angela Hudson picked her way across the potholed high school parking lot. In early August, the summer break wasn't over yet, and the lot was empty save three other cars.

The other three schmucks who'd been wrangled into joining the reunion committee. Schmucks, because who wanted this job? No one.

She'd been too nice to hang up on the high school principal when he'd called and pleaded for her to take a spot on the committee.

It wasn't that she didn't have the time. She was a busy single mother with a cake decorating business, but she could carve out an hour or two out of her schedule.

It was the humiliation factor.

She'd been homecoming queen. Head cheerleader. Voted by her classmates as *Most Likely to Succeed*.

Ten years later, and she was a failure. Failed

marriage. Failed relationship with her own dad. Failed business—or close enough.

And she really didn't want to walk in and face off with three former classmates who probably had it all together.

But she also wasn't one to back out when she'd committed to doing something, so she straightened her shoulders and the cuffs on her Anne Klein blouse and pushed inside the dim, cool building.

Why they'd chosen to meet here instead of someplace like the coffee shop Cup of Joe on the town's small Main Street was a mystery.

Sounded like they were all here already as voices echoed down the shadowed hallway. Someone had left the overhead lights off, and sunlight from the bank of windows at the front of the building angled along the floor before disappearing. One of the classroom lights was on, spilling out of the room and onto the floor.

She braced herself and sucked in her tummy before passing through the door.

"Angela!"

"Hi!"

A chorus of female voices rang out. She was momentarily blinded as her eyes adjusted to the overhead fluorescents.

"Mary Beth. Jo." Angela nodded to the music teacher and to the UPS store owner. Both women were local to Ross, Oklahoma, population two thousand forty-three, though Angela mostly greeted them in passing and hadn't had a real conversation with them in years. Real conversation meant admitting to the imperfect status of her life.

"And Morgan. I haven't seen you since graduation."

Morgan had been in a vastly different social circle than Angela's popular cheerleader friends back in high school. Though she'd occasionally crossed paths with Mary Beth and Jo, Angela realized she didn't know anything at all about the other woman.

Back then, Morgan had been voted *Most likely to leave town and never come back*, and she had. She didn't look entirely happy to be here now, chin propped on her hand with a glum expression.

Awkwardness descended, and Angela let her eyes roam the room. It was a math classroom, the chalkboard she remembered now replaced with a white board, but the linoleum and desks seemed to be the very same from ten years ago. Everything had seemed bright, important and life-or-death back then. Now the classroom looked tired and faded. Or maybe it was her jaded eyes.

"So we all got roped into the committee?" Angela tried to inject some brightness into her voice, but it felt false. Like her smile. "Are we waiting on anyone else?"

"I don't think so," Mary Beth said.

Morgan tapped a pencil on the desk. "Principal Jay said there were four of us who volunteered."

Volunteered...yeah. Sure.

"Let's get down to it then," Jo said, flipping open a binder. "I need to get back to the store soon."

They worked together relatively well, quickly deciding on a theme, assigning tasks for contacting vendors and classmates, and scheduling their next meeting for a month from now.

Angela couldn't help sighing, glancing out the window.

"What?" Jo asked.

Angela debated whether to say what she was thinking. She shrugged. "I'm not sure I even want to go to the reunion."

Morgan's eyes flicked up from where she'd been staring at the desk. "You too?"

Mary Beth glanced between them, wearing a bemused smile. "What's the big deal?"

"Nothing for you," Angela said. "You've got a boyfriend. I have an ex, and a failing business, and I'm not looking forward to making small talk with everyone who'll want to catch up."

"Tell me about it," Morgan agreed.

Mary Beth looked to Jo. "What about you?"

Jo nodded slowly. "I never thought I'd still be single by our ten-year." Some shadow passed behind her eyes, one that Angela couldn't recognize. She vaguely remembered a prayer request from Bible class. Had Jo battled some illness? Was that why she was still single?

"Too bad we can't just manufacture boyfriends for the occasion," Morgan muttered.

Angela snorted. Wouldn't that be nice? "I wish."

"You could," Mary Beth said. "What about online dating?"

Angela froze, watching to see that Jo and Morgan had done the same.

Mary Beth went on. "If all you're looking for is a date for the reunion, why not? Maybe it could even be more."

Angela's mind spun faster than a mixer on high speed. She'd resisted dating since her divorce, knowing her baggage was a lot to take. But if a guy knew the whole sordid tale up front because he'd read her profile...maybe it could work.

"I'm up for it," she blurted.

"I...might," Jo said.

All three turned to Morgan, who blushed.

"C'mon," Angela said. "If we both do it, you have to participate."

"What about Mary Beth? She has an out," Morgan protested.

Mary Beth shrugged. "If, by some tiny chance, things don't work out between me and Todd, I'll sign up for a dating site."

Angela and Jo turned back to Morgan with raised brows. They waited her out until she huffed. "Fine. Can we please get back to business now?"

The meeting broke up soon after. Each woman had been assigned reunion tasks to complete before their next meeting.

As Angela walked across the parking lot back to her car, she felt a slight stirring of hope. What if she could find someone again? There were plenty of nights she went to bed lonely, remembering the camaraderie, the feeling of belonging, before everything had gone wrong with Rob.

Maybe she *could* find that again. Was online dating the answer? She'd promised to try, and for the first time in a long time, she was open to life again.

CHAPTER ONE

What are the most important qualities you're looking for in a match?
SenseiSam: "I'm looking for a girl who's fun-loving, pretty, and athletic."

"And I was the youngest partner in the history of the company."

Angela dredged up a smile, knowing it must be reflecting her feelings. She wasn't that good at hiding them.

This was a disaster.

Sam L. Peterson, Esquire—aka SenseiSam—didn't seem to notice. He was still going on about his important work and his eighty hour workweeks for an Oklahoma City law firm.

She'd promised herself she wouldn't fall for someone climbing the corporate ladder again. Not that there was much chance of falling for this guy.

When he took a breath, she jumped in. "Well,"

she said as brightly as she could, "thanks for meeting me."

His mouth opened as she stood from the table for two in the small but busy coffee shop. She wanted to walk straight out, but she couldn't. Thad was at a table in the corner, poring over a coloring book.

Sam said, "But—"

"I think if we're both honest with ourselves, this isn't a perfect match." She couldn't bear another minute with him, but she made herself smile anyway.

He looked perplexed, but then nodded slowly. She waited until he'd gone before she joined Thad in the corner booth that nearly swallowed him up. A deep breath brought a small sense of calm and the pungent aroma of coffee beans. Afternoon sunlight slanted through the window and warmed them slightly.

"You okay, buddy?" she asked.

"Mmhmm." Thad was her seven-year-old pride and joy. He was completely focused on a coloring page, his chestnut head bent low as he filled in the superhero's shield with blue crayon, careful to stay in the lines.

A shadow fell over the table. "One cinnamon roll," said a male voice.

Angela looked up to see the shop's owner, Wes, set a white plate in front of Thad. On the plate was the biggest cinnamon roll she'd ever seen. It was steaming, and the scents of cinnamon and sugar wafted to her.

"I didn't order that," she said, even though her mouth was watering. She aimed a look at her son. "Thad?"

He affected an innocent look. One she didn't buy.

Wes crossed his arms, and she realized this man wasn't Wes at all, though they shared the same dark hair and movie-star good looks.

This version of Wes had a tattooed sleeve from his right wrist all the way up his arm until it disappeared into his T-shirt. Had Wes's shoulders ever been that broad beneath his red apron? And then her eyes tracked to his face, noticing the dangerous five o'clock shadow and the small scar that bisected one dark eyebrow.

"Are you Wes's brother?"

His gaze didn't change at the impertinent question. How did someone cultivate a poker face like that? "His twin," he finally said. "I'm Drew."

Drew. He raised one eyebrow at her—the one with the scar—and she blushed, realizing she was still staring.

"I'm Thad," piped her son.

"Yeah, I got that. And your mom is...?" Somehow his gaze remained on Thad, but she felt his focus shift to her with an almost tangible touch.

"Angela." Thad went back to his artwork, attention span met.

Which left the tattooed barista free to shift that steely blue gaze back to her.

She cleared her throat. "I didn't know Wes had a twin. Where are you from?"

"NYC. Just down for the summer to help my brother."

Something shifted behind his eyes as he said the words, and curiosity piqued in Angela's gut. Not that it was any of her business. So she tried to stifle it.

"You gonna pay for the bun or not?" Drew's chin jerked to the cinnamon roll still sitting on the table between Angela and Thad. She'd like to say she'd forgotten all about it, but the smells still had her mouth watering for the sugary, cinnamony confection.

Angela leveled a look on her son. "Thad?"

Thad's eyes darted up from his drawing. "Please, Mom?"

The man shifted. He was impossible to ignore, not that she was trying all that hard.

"I think you're supposed to ask your ma *before* you order," Drew said. He reached for the plate.

Thad's shoulders slumped.

Angela touched the barista's wrist before he

touched the plate. Heat streaked up her arm at the contact, and he jumped, pulling his arm back.

She swallowed hard. "We'll keep it. Sorry for the trouble."

His lips firmed in a line, and he stepped away from the table.

"You didn't like that guy?"

It took her longer than it should've to make sense of Thad's question, probably because her eyes had tracked Drew's progress behind the counter. She shook herself out of the daze of...*attraction?*...and focused back on her son, who was peeling away the first layer of flaky cinnamon roll.

"Hey!"

He gave her a cheeky grin even as he popped the piece in his mouth, smearing icing across his upper lip. The moment squeezed her heart. This was a hint of the little boy she hadn't seen often since Christmas break when Thad's best friend had moved out of state.

She huffed and grabbed her own sticky bite off the roll. "SenseiSam was too self-absorbed. And he had a demanding job."

Thad nodded, still chewing. He looked out the window. Outside, a group of adults and kids crossed the street headed for the Cup of Joe.

Was he thinking about his father? Rob had been absent from their lives even before the separation and divorce. Angela had done her best to keep things together, fighting a losing battle for far longer than she probably should've. It wasn't that she was a perfectionist. She just hated failing. She had been nominated *Most Likely to Succeed* in high school, after all.

The truth was, she'd chosen her husband badly, and now Thad was paying the price, dealing with a father who was content to see his son one or two weekends a year.

Thad jumped up from his seat. "I gotta use the restroom."

He disappeared around the corner of a small hallway leading off of the rear of the coffee shop. She'd been in enough to know there was no outside access back there, only the separate single stall men's and women's restrooms, so she felt reasonably sure he was safe. He was almost eight. She had to cut the apron strings a little more as he grew.

Sometimes she just felt so inadequate to raise a boy by herself. Like lately, when she knew there was something wrong, but he wouldn't tell her what.

She sighed, popping another bite of cinnamon roll in her mouth. The sugary confection made her thirsty, and she hadn't ordered coffee during her terrible date. Had that been foresight? Or had some part of her known she'd chicken out?

It didn't matter. She wasn't interested in falling for someone with a corporate job, not after Rob.

Thad seemed to be taking his sweet time, so she stood and approached the counter. There were no other customers in line, and she felt self-conscious, as if she were a teenager chasing a cute guy.

From behind the counter, Drew waited, palms flat on the surface.

"Could I have a tall caramel macchiato?" She pushed a twenty-dollar bill across the counter, plenty to cover the drink and the pastry.

"Sure thing." He wasn't exactly smiling, but he wasn't frowning, either. Had the impromptu touch affected him as much as it had her?

He turned to start making the drink, and because there were no other customers and because she hated awkward silences—even with the machine whirring and spitting—she blurted the first question she thought of.

"So what do you do back in New York?"

He glanced over his shoulder. "How do you know I'm not a full time barista?"

Somehow, she knew better. Wes owned this place, but Drew seemed like someone who... She couldn't put her finger on it.

"You're not an aspiring rock star or something?"

He laughed, a sharp bark of sound that

appeared to surprise him as much as it surprised her.

He turned, liquid sloshing in her paper cup, and moved to pour the foam. One corner of his mouth ticked up. "Definitely not a rock star, aspiring or otherwise."

He snapped a lid on her drink and slid it across the counter. "What do you do?"

She crossed her arms but then realized she had to pick up the cup, so she managed an awkward shift and ended up with one hand on her hip and the other grasping the cup. "No fair. I'm not telling if you don't."

He smirked. "You think I can't find out in about ten minutes in a town this small?"

She shrugged. "You can try." It was a bluff, and they both knew it. Everyone in Ross knew about her home-based baking business, though no one knew how close she was to bankruptcy.

The bell over the door rang, and several people trooped in. Angela couldn't monopolize his time when he had customers.

She raised her cup in salute. "Thanks."

He nodded, already focused on the line building behind her.

Thad was peering around the corner. He caught sight of her, and his gaze darted around the inside of the coffee shop before he returned to the table.

"You'd better finish this," she told him, pushing the cinnamon roll in front of him.

He shoved the remaining half in his mouth.

"Thad!" she chided half-laughing, half in horror. He was such a boy!

They picked up their trash, and she took the remainder of her coffee with her.

She couldn't help sending one last look to the handsome barista. He was waiting on a customer, but his eyes lifted and met hers briefly before the door closed behind her.

CHAPTER TWO

What are you most passionate about?
ThursDave: "Mature chicks."

Saturday night, Drew Scheffield grabbed a medium-sized round tray from behind the counter and made a slow circuit around the coffeehouse, picking up trash and plates that had been discarded or set aside.

It was humid, packed with bodies, thanks to his brother's genius marketing idea to do a superhero night. Their customers were a mix of families and singles, conversing about DC, Marvel, and everything else superhero. Some people had even come in costume. Who knew Ross, Oklahoma, would support this kind of nightlife?

Drew could've done without the leather-covered Catwoman who kept shooting him not-so-covert glances.

He couldn't help his awareness of Angela

Hudson. He'd known the moment she walked in. She was now ensconced at one of the corner round tables across from a good looking, slightly younger guy in a superman outfit. Tights, gelled hair and all. People kept tripping on the guy's cape.

But that wasn't the reason Drew wanted to get rid of the guy. It was because Angela kept leaning toward him, her entire focus on him, those caramel-colored, endless eyes, absorbed in rapt attention. Her chestnut hair, a match for her son's, kept falling over her shoulder, and Drew was mesmerized by the way she pushed it behind her ear.

Drew had no reason for the jealousy that swept through him. He didn't even know Angela. And he really didn't need a complication in his life. He was leaving in six weeks, heading back to NYC and the life he'd put on hold there. He'd only meant to be gone for the summer, but now summer had turned to fall.

He needed the extra weeks to catch his breath. Find his footing. He did not need a distraction.

But there was no stopping the way his heart leapt when Angela had walked in the door tonight, the way every hair on the back of his neck stood to attention when he passed by her chair on his route back to the tiny kitchen behind the bar. He ducked through the door.

He really didn't need this. Wasn't looking for any kind of relationship, not after what had happened with Jennifer.

He disposed of the trash and deposited the dirty plates in the huge industrial sink. Man, he wasn't getting out of here until the wee hours with that many dishes waiting on him after closing. When he returned to the front, the crowd had finally begun to thin, and for once, the line of customers had dwindled to zero.

And Angela's date had disappeared.

Drew's brother Wes was a penny-pincher and had given explicit instructions, so Drew let the second barista go home. Drew would do the closing and be back here far too early tomorrow morning.

It might have felt like Wes was taking advantage of him if Drew hadn't asked for the hours. Knocking around in Wes's large farmhouse outside of town left too much room for thinking. Thinking led to remembering, remembering led to grief.

Drew would rather work, even though he'd left NYC to take a break from his high-intensity job on Wall Street.

He pulled a double shot espresso. Wiped down the counter again. People continued to filter out of the shop.

Angela approached and took a seat at one of

the four bar stools that lined the counter.

He told himself to stay away, but his feet carried him the short distance anyway. "Need anything?"

She looked up, and he instantly saw the exhaustion he'd missed when he'd passed her earlier. Tiny lines fanned from her eyes, and her smile seemed fragile. She swept her hair behind her ear.

"How about a cup of hot tea?" she asked.

He rummaged behind the counter and then handed her the basket of tea bags to look through while he filled a mug with steaming water.

He told himself to set it on the counter and go back to cleaning up but instead found himself leaning on his elbows, much too close.

"Superman didn't do it for you?" Maybe it was cruel to bring it up, but this was the second date he'd seen end prematurely. Maybe she had really high standards.

She winced. "Did you see how young he was? He might've still been in college. He *definitely* lied about his age on his profile."

That stopped Drew short. "Wait a minute. You're online dating?"

She glared at him and wrinkled her nose and looked so adorable that he had to swallow hard.

"Don't judge," she said. "A couple of friends

and I made this pact to find our special someones online before our ten-year high school reunion next spring. Did you go to yours?"

The memory of Jennifer in the red cocktail dress hit him, and it was a moment before he could clear his throat. "Yeah, I went."

She noticed. Her head tilted slightly, and there was just enough of a pause to make him think she was going to give in to her curiosity and ask about his reaction. But she didn't.

"Yeah, so... I was the girl voted most likely to succeed."

He grinned. He could see that. "Homecoming queen?"

She blushed.

That was interesting. She'd brought up the high school reunion. He couldn't help but wonder if she was one of those people who considered the "good ol' days" the best of their lives.

"Life didn't turn out like I thought it would. In a lot of ways." She said the words to the countertop, rubbing at a water-stained spot with one index finger.

"I'd guess every person in your graduating class feels the same way," he said. "Nothing to be ashamed of if you don't have a date."

Her chin lifted. Stubborn. "Oh, I'll have a date. There can't be that many yahoos in the online dating scene, can there?"

She winced again. "That felt like I jinxed it."

"Somebody like you isn't going to have any issues finding a date." And *that* sounded like flirting. Just what he did not need to be doing.

The man in a Wolverine T-shirt next to her got up and left, giving Drew a chance to pick up the trash there and wipe down that spot. He focused on the empty spot instead of on her.

"Yes, because single moms are all the rage," she said.

It was a huge target, an invitation that made him want to reply that he liked single moms just fine, but he clamped his lips shut. A two-a-day patron shouted a goodbye before pushing through the door and gave him a reprieve.

She fiddled with the handle of her tea mug. "Plus, I'd...well, I'd like to find more than just a date."

He knew what she was going to say before the words emerged.

"I miss being half of a pair. Having someone to tag-team with when Thad has soccer practice and the pantry is empty and I need to go to the store. Having adult conversation at the supper table."

Lying in bed late at night, whispering about their day. Lazy Saturday morning breakfasts. Listening to her sing while she cleaned house. She couldn't carry a tune to save her life.

A visceral pang of longing and grief hit him square in the solar plexus, and he hurriedly bent behind the counter to hide suddenly wet eyes. He knocked around several glasses, hoping the sound of their clinking together would make her think he was sorting down here and not hiding.

He knew it was impossible, but he wanted Jennifer back. Her death hadn't been sudden, but it had still left a gaping hole inside of him. His chest felt tight, but he couldn't afford a panic attack, not having sent home the other barista and with several customers still loitering. Not to mention Angela.

He counted slowly to ten, focusing on slowing his breathing and the staccato beat of his heart. It didn't work, not really, but he couldn't stay down here any longer.

He straightened, forcing a smile that he was sure she could see through. She saw too much.

Sure enough, her eyes searched his face before she looked down at her cup, fiddling with the handle again.

"I'm sure that's TMI about me," she said. "What about you? How soon do you go back to New York and your career as a music teacher?"

Her words were a distraction he sorely needed, and he was able to make his smile more genuine. "Another six weeks. And I'm not a music teacher.

What is it about me that makes you think I'm musical?"

She tilted her head to one side, a lock of hair falling in her eyes. She flicked it away impatiently. "I don't know." Her eyes lingered on his arms, his tats. Was that it? But then she glanced up at his hair, his face.

He found himself warming under her frank perusal.

"Maybe it's how you look. Not musical, huh?"

"Not a bone in my entire body." Jennifer hadn't been the only one who couldn't carry a tune.

"You could just tell me what you do."

He moved to end of the counter. "And ruin my air of mystique?" He knew she could easily ask Wes when his twin was in the shop, but for whatever reason, he liked this game.

She took a last swig of her tea and stood. "I guess I should go. My babysitter is going to turn back into a pumpkin."

"Same time next week?" he asked. He didn't know why, hadn't meant for the words to pop out. Her dating schedule was her own business.

"Probably. I've still got a few lines in the water." And one of these times she was going to reel in a winner who saw what a jewel she was. Drew knew it was only a matter of time.

"Good luck," he offered as she headed for the

door.

"Thanks," she called back. "I'm sure I'll need it."

CHAPTER THREE

What are five things you can't live without?
Tarzan3.0: "Motocross, ESPN, puppies, my favorite sweatshirt, my mom's home cooking."

On Saturday, midmorning sun slanted across the parking lot and glared off windshields. Angela sat inside the coffee shop at a table next to the window, so she could see Thad where she'd left him at the small city park across the street. She shivered, even with a sweater on, because even though it was a cool autumn morning, the shop was still running its A/C. Her mouth watered from the scents of someone's crisp apple pastry.

She wouldn't have brought Thad along, but her babysitter had cancelled, and Angela had been looking forward to this date. At the park, he wasn't really unsupervised, because she was watching. He was seven, plenty big enough to play by himself for half an hour or so.

She refused to be disappointed that Drew wasn't on shift this morning. She was here to see Jimmy.

Although, who called himself *Jimmy*, instead of *James* or *Jim*? It seemed like a childhood nickname that you'd leave behind.

The man who slid into the booth across from her was definitely *not* a kid. Broad shoulders and a great physique were the first things she noticed. He wasn't bad looking, with pleasant features, clear blue eyes. His nose looked like it had been broken before.

"Hey," he said, with a wide, easy smile.

"Hi. I'm Angela." She stuck her hand over the table, and they shook. His touch was just right—not too girly and not too hard of a squeeze.

His smile widened. "Jimmy." He had straight, white teeth. Probably he'd worn braces.

He definitely smiled more than Drew. And why was she thinking about Drew again?

"Thanks for meeting me so early," he said. "I just got off a twenty-four-hour shift at the fire department, and I usually go home and crash. I would've hated to have to wait until my next four-day break to meet you."

Well, that was charming.

With Jimmy sitting where he was, she could see past his shoulder to where Thad was playing and still appear to be attentive. Right now Thad was standing on the top level of the huge wooden fort. Looked like he might be about to slide.

"I saw on your profile you work at a bakery?" Jimmy said.

"I actually own the business. I have two industrial ovens in my kitchen, and work from home."

"Awesome. So you get to set your own schedule and stuff."

Yes. But that meant she had a hard time turning it off. Every time she walked through the kitchen, she was reminded of the upcoming bills and worried about whether she had enough jobs for the month. She'd had two referrals last month, which meant she'd been able to pay the mortgage and an overdue water bill and breathe a little.

Over Jimmy's shoulder, she saw two other boys approach Thad, who'd raced to the bottom of the slide. One of them got in Thad's face, rousing her protective instincts.

Jimmy was still talking. "—favorite thing to bake? I'm partial to—"

"I'm sorry," she interrupted, coming out of her seat as the second boy closed in and the first one shoved Thad. "My son..."

She was out the door before the words were out.

"Son?" Jimmy's voice cut off as the door closed behind her.

She ran out in the street without looking. There was no traffic, thank God. The three boys were in an all-out tussle now, Thad on the bottom. She wanted to shout, but her voice seemed to stick in her throat. Were her feet even moving? She felt as if she were running through a thick pound cake batter.

And then, as she finally crossed over the curb into the grass, help arrived in the form of a tall, imposing figure cutting across the sidewalk. With a recognizable tattoo on his arm.

"Hey!" Drew shouted. His dark boots kicked up wood chips as he approached the trio of boys at a jog.

The two other boys looked up and then ran off, leaving Thad prone on the ground.

"Thad!" Her gasp brought her boy's head turning toward her.

She and Drew reached him at the same time. Thad sat up with a groan.

"Hey, man," Drew greeted softly. "Take it easy, why don'cha?"

She wasn't so laid back, especially when she saw the trickle of blood beneath Thad's nose. "Baby, what happened?" She reached for her son, but Thad scooted back, hands digging into the wood chips as he scrabbled away.

"Leave me alone!" He stood up, wiping one hand beneath his nose. It came away bloody.

"Thad!" She reached for him again, but he turned and ran.

She started to follow, but Drew grabbed her arm. "Give him a second to cool off."

She yanked out of his grasp. "Are you a parent?" she demanded. She knew it was rude, but her emotions were flying high, and that was her *baby*!

Something passed behind his eyes. "No, but I've been a boy. Look"—Drew pointed—"he's sitting beneath that tree right over there. He didn't run off."

She had to lean down to see below the fort's structure. Looking through the opening, she could see Thad hunched in a miserable ball at the base of a gnarled old oak that shaded the park during the summer.

"He's okay," Drew said.

"How do you know?" There was her demanding, worried Mama-bear voice again. "His nose was bleeding—"

"It was already drying up."

"He might have broken ribs, I think they were punching him—"

"He doesn't have broken ribs."

"And what if he gets a punctured lung or something?"

Drew leveled a look at her. She might've exaggerated with that last one, but she was near tears.

"He's fine," Drew said.

"Uh, Angela—?"

At the unexpected voice, she whirled around. Jimmy stood on the curb, his expression closed. A complete one-eighty from how he'd appeared in the coffee shop earlier.

She'd completely forgotten about him, about their date.

With a glance at Thad—she couldn't look at Drew right now—she walked the few steps over to her date.

He rubbed the back of his neck. The movement showed off his nice biceps, but he wasn't looking her in the eye anymore. "I, uh... didn't realize you had a kid."

"What?" She hadn't meant to blurt the thought aloud. Her mind was spinning with worries for her son, and she was having a hard time registering the meaning behind Jimmy's comment. "It was on my profile. Right at the top." She'd made sure it was, so potential dates would know she was a single mom.

"Look, it's a deal-breaker for me. No kids. I'm really sorry."

She knew her mouth was hanging open.

He had the grace to look sheepish.

She couldn't deal with him or his *no kids* philosophy right now. Her son needed her. "Thanks for letting me know." She knew the words were sharp—she felt jagged and broken inside right now, so that's what came out.

He nodded and turned away.

Drew was still there when she turned around. His face revealed nothing, though she knew he had to have heard that entire conversation with Jimmy.

She tried to pretend he wasn't there, started to march right past him to get to Thad.

But Drew caught her arm again.

A wave of exhaustion and emotion rocked her, and this time she didn't have the strength to pull away.

"Just give him a minute," Drew said. He nudged her toward one of the swings that hung beneath a branch of the fort.

Her knees had started trembling, and she sank into the seat. It pinched her rear and thighs—made for kids, not adults—but the chains gave her something to hold onto, and she clung.

A hot knot clogged her throat. She tried to clear it away. "Two years ago, he wouldn't have run away from me." Tears blurred her vision, and she let go of one of the chains to press her thumb and forefinger into her closed eyes. Maybe that would stem the tide.

Two years ago, she and Thad's father had still been together. Her son had been a brand-new, bright-eyed kindergartener, and he'd run to her with every little problem, every skinned knee, every paper cut. Now he ran away.

She'd failed her marriage, and now she was failing Thad.

With only one hand steadying her, and her eyes closed, she wobbled on the swing. Drew clasped her shoulder. Steadied her.

"You won't always be able to fight his battles for him," Drew said in low tones. "Besides, those two punks are hanging out in front of the drugstore across the street and watching him to see what happens. You don't want to give him a rep as a mama's boy."

She didn't?

Somehow, Drew's presence helped. She took a deep breath, then another, and finally was able to open her eyes without shedding the tears. She'd keep them bottled until late tonight and give them to her pillow then, when Thad was asleep.

"I'm going to talk to him," Drew said. "You mind?"

She shook her head. She couldn't give Thad his father. Maybe Drew could say something that would help.

His footsteps crunched in the mulch as he walked away.

She watched him sit on the ground next to her son. Where had he even come from? He hadn't been at the coffee shop. Maybe he was arriving at work and had seen the altercation from the employee parking lot off to the side of the shop. That would explain how he'd cut across the grass and sidewalk.

Their voices carried to her.

"You okay?" Drew asked.

"Yeah." Thad didn't look at the man beside him, just played with a blade of grass, using it like a tiny sword to hit the other grasses near his leg.

"You know those guys?"

Thad nodded.

"They go to your school?"

"Yeah."

"This the first time they've picked on you?"

A beat.

And then Thad shook his head slowly.

She began to tremble. Thad had been bullied, and she hadn't known about it? Had she been too wrapped up in her own problems, the business, this dating thing, to notice?

"What's their problem?" Drew asked.

Thad shrugged.

But Drew waited with just the right amount of patience.

"They saw me crying in class once before school got out for the summer. And now they keep calling me crybaby." Thad swished the grass sword through the grass with a little more violence now.

"What happened in class?"

Thad sighed. "At Christmas, my best friend Jack moved away. All the way to Ohio. Our favorite class together was art, and our teacher always let us be partners. Then after Jack was gone, there was this paper mache project that he would have loved, but I had to have a *girl* as my partner, and it just made me sad."

She gripped the swing chains until her knuckles were white. She'd known he missed Jack. The two boys had been inseparable since preschool, but Jack's family had relocated due to a job situation. She'd let Thad video-chat with his friend as often as he wanted. She hadn't realized her son was still so upset about his friend's departure.

"I'm sorry." Drew didn't try to over-analyze the situation or patronize Thad. He simply reached over and ruffled her boy's hair. "Some guys might thing crying is a baby thing, but I don't."

Thad looked up at him, and Angela saw the admiration in her son's expression. "Really?"

Drew's voice was serious and weighted. "Really."

Thad sniffed and ran his hand beneath his

nose again. She was relieved to see that the bleeding had stopped. The blows must not have been that bad. "Maybe I should go talk to my mom."

Drew nodded. "She's probably going to freak out a little."

"I know."

They both stood and brushed dead leaves and grass from their pants.

She tried really hard not to *freak out*, but she couldn't help a little sniffle of her own when Thad came to her for a hug.

Drew was still there as they crossed the street and she loaded Thad into the backseat of her Ford Explorer. She shut the door and turned to the man who'd shown up at just the right moment.

"Thanks for your help. For making sure he was okay, and..." For talking to him when she couldn't. But the words stuck in her throat. She cleared it. "It's been a rough eighteen months on him. First his dad left, and then Jack moved... So, just...thanks."

His eyes were intent, and she brushed some of her hair behind her ear. No telling what she looked like. Probably like herself, a windblown, harried working mom doing the best she could.

But he kept looking. And she started to get uncomfortable. And started rambling. "I probably should've just cancelled the date when my babysitter called to tell me she had a stomach bug. But I thought he'd be fine for a little while in the park—I was watching him."

He cupped her elbow briefly to stem her words, his presence steady. "Next time your babysitter cancels, call me."

CHAPTER FOUR

What are you looking for in a relationship?
Lionheart: "I'm looking for someone special. I'll know her when I find her."

This might not have been the best idea.

Drew was elbow-deep in a sink full of dishes when he heard the garage door at Angela's place kick on.

He'd offered to babysit Thad for her next date, but he hadn't really thought she'd take him up on it.

He'd been shocked when she'd called, but since he'd been off from the coffee shop that night, he'd agreed. Thad was a great kid, reminded Drew a lot of his brother Wes as a child, methodical and even-tempered. Drew had been a slob with a quick temper.

When he'd volunteered for this, he definitely hadn't thought through how messy kids were and the cleanup a couple hours with one would entail.

He also hadn't thought about what it would feel like knowing Angela was out with another guy.

Apparently the date had gone well, because she'd been gone more than two hours. That was a lot of *getting to know you.*

And he definitely wasn't jealous. Had no right to be and no business nosing into her life. He just had a stomachache from all the brownies he and Thad had eaten earlier. He'd kept the kid to two, but he'd binged after the boy was in bed, ignoring the judgmental glances from their adolescent golden retriever. He refused to feel guilty because of a dog.

Her house was like her, open, airy, dressed in warm colors. The kind of home you wanted to return to at the end of the day.

So where was she?

On the heels of that thought, she came through the door, head turned back as she closed the garage door. She was sliding her purse off her shoulder when she caught sight of him standing at the sink.

"What are you doing?"

He thought it was pretty obvious, but he held up the dishrag and a pot covered in suds, dripping into the sink. "Dishes."

She set her purse on the far end of the counter, well away from the mess of cocoa and flour spread across the granite. It looked like a brownie mix bomb had gone off in the center of the room. Which it kind of had. The dog had licked up several blobs.

"I'll get the counters next and sweep real quick before I head out." It wasn't her mess, after all.

But she looked completely confused. "What happened here? Somebody murder one of my bags of flour?"

"Something like that. Thad wanted to cook supper, and then of course we had to do something for dessert, so...brownies."

"I left supper in the fridge. Leftovers."

He pulled a face to show her what he thought of that. He could've waited to eat until he made it back to Wes's place tonight, but he couldn't let the poor kid suffer like that.

He hand-dried the pot and set it on the towel he'd put out on the counter, where the rest of the pots and pans and utensils they'd used now rested. He moved to unplug the sink.

"We have a dishwasher," she said. She was still standing where she'd stopped, like she was in shock or something.

"Your pots are so fancy, I wasn't sure they could go in there. They're clean now anyway."

He wiped down the counter.

She laughed a little, but the sound was desperate. "So you made dinner with my son. And now you're cleaning up." She made it sound like a question, but he didn't get it.

He shrugged. It wasn't a big deal. "We made the mess. I probably should've made him help, but he was worn out after we played catch in the backyard." For over an hour. Drew was a little worn out himself. His shoulder was aching from all the long bombs Thad had demanded he throw. And they had a huge backyard.

He was focused on scrubbing off a caked-on spot of batter but heard her mumble, "Not a big deal to clean up after himself."

Had her husband been one of those losers who insisted that only a woman could do kitchen work?

"And you're not by any chance a janitor in New York City?"

He laughed. "No."

She opened a full-sized pantry door and pulled out a broom. He'd had a good chuckle at her pantry earlier. Everything was organized and in its place, all the labels facing forward and every can lined up like little soldiers. Thad wasn't the only methodical one. Drew had itched to move some things around, but he'd controlled himself. Barely.

"You're very domestic for a bachelor." She didn't look at him as she swept up the crumbs and flour they'd left on the floor. "Why aren't you married?"

He'd known his marital status might come up, but somehow he could never prepare himself for the hit. He took it, lost his breath at the momentary pain in his gut. "I was."

She stilled.

He was aware of her stare but kept his focus on scrubbing away the countertop mess. It seemed like he was getting nowhere. "My wife passed away late last year."

Saying the words still made him feel as if he were scuba diving and his air had run out. One hundred feet deep and drowning. It still seemed surreal. It couldn't be real, could it? Wasn't he going to wake up from this nightmare and find Jennifer in bed right beside him?

But he didn't wake up—he never did—and she was still gone. And he still ached, all over, because he'd lost her.

"I'm so sorry." He heard the soft catch in her voice but couldn't look up, because if she had tears in her eyes, he'd lose it.

He cleared his throat and kept scrubbing, praying she'd just go back to sweeping the floor. He needed to escape.

Wes had probably saved his life, asking him to come down for the summer and help with the coffee shop. He'd been drowning, going through the motions of his old life, but without Jennifer, every day was an endless black hole. Learning the job of a barista had given him something to focus on, kept his hands and mind busy.

Now, he searched for a distraction. Grasped on to the first thing he could think of. "How was the date? Seems like it must've been better than the last couple." Or else it wouldn't have lasted so long.

"He was very nice."

He winced. Nice. The death knell.

"We had a lot to talk about, but I think we both felt like we'd be better friends than anything else."

He kept her in his peripheral vision. She swept her small pile of debris into the dustpan and then dumped that into the trash canister. He rinsed the rag in the sink.

He'd squeezed out the extra water and draped it over the center separator in the two sinks. He was turning to tell her goodbye, but she must've been passing behind him to return the broom to its place.

She stopped short, but they ended up face to face. Too close. With his emotions already in chaos, looking down at her was dangerous. Her eyes were clear and soft, her cheeks slightly flushed.

She was imminently kissable.

"There was just no attraction," she breathed. "You know?"

She was talking about her date, but he couldn't stop staring. The air between them seemed thick and almost humming with anticipation.

No, he didn't know what it felt like not to be attracted to Angela.

Her lashes lowered over her expressive eyes, and the moment shattered.

He stepped back, bumping his side into the counter. The physical pain brought clarity. What was he doing? It was like his brain had switched off.

He might be attracted to her, but he didn't want to be.

He rubbed the back of his neck. "I need to go."

She seemed flustered, her hands fluttering in front of her. "Okay. Yes. Thank you for staying with Thad."

He wasn't sure if he even nodded in his haste to get out of there.

Ten minutes later, he sat in his car in front of Wes's place, still too shaken up to go in. His brother was home, the lights were on, and Wes would take one look at him and know something was up.

How could he explain what was going on when he couldn't even understand it himself?

How could he be attracted to Angela when he was still so deep in grief over Jennifer's death?

But it turned out he was wrong about Wes being inside. His brother approached the car from behind and knocked on Drew's window.

Drew opened the door.

"Where have you been?" Wes asked.

"Out. Babysitting," he amended not wanting his brother to get the wrong idea.

"Funny thing. Cassandra said she'd seen you flirting with one of the single moms that comes into the coffee shop all the time."

Drew grimaced. "It's not like that."

"What is it like?"

Drew closed his eyes. "I don't really want to talk about it." He pressed his thumb and forefinger into his eyes, but the ache behind them didn't abate.

He couldn't be attracted to Angela. He wouldn't allow it.

"You know, it's okay to move on."

"It doesn't feel okay!" Drew burst out of the car. He paced several feet away and then whirled back on his brother.

"It feels like I'm betraying her."

Wes waited, balancing on the balls of his feet as if he thought Drew might be inclined to throw a punch. That might actually help him release some of his pent-up emotions.

"She's gone, man," Wes said.

"It hasn't been that long." Drew ran an

agitated hand through his hair.

Even though it felt like it had been forever.

Wes shrugged. "The heart wants what it wants. Just because it's only been a few months doesn't mean it's too soon to start falling for someone again.

"I'm not falling for her," Drew burst out.

"You keep telling yourself that." Wes slapped Drew on the shoulder and headed toward the house, leaving Drew out in the dark night.

He looked up at the stars for a long time, but there were no answers there.

CHAPTER FIVE

Other than appearance, what is the first thing that people notice about you?
HubbaBubba3: "My manly smell."

Lunchtime on Saturday, Angela sat again at one of those small round tables in the coffee shop.

Her mother had Thad for the weekend. Later this afternoon, Angela would be putting the finishing touches on a wedding cake she'd spent all evening yesterday working on.

After she delivered it this evening, she would start on a huge batch of cupcakes for a bridal shower tomorrow afternoon. The work was a good distraction, but her date was late, and it was hard to keep her mind focused on that and not on the man behind the counter.

She'd gone five days without seeing Drew. She hadn't wanted to make things awkward for him, and action on her online profile was slow until today's date had messaged her.

She couldn't stop thinking about those moments in her kitchen when she'd thought Drew might kiss her.

She would've kissed him back if he'd done it. She was attracted to him. She'd thought he was attracted to her, but now that she knew about his late wife, she wasn't so sure.

All those tiny things she'd seen suddenly started to make sense. When she'd talked about missing a partner, having someone to do little things with, he'd ducked behind the bar. She'd thought he was working or maybe just barely listening to her. But had he been hiding his upsetting emotions? On the night of the almost-kiss, she'd seen his feelings, even though he hadn't looked at her directly. They'd been there in the ticking muscle in his jaw, the set of his shoulders, and his jerky motions. He was still deeply grieving for his wife, that much was obvious.

She didn't know what to do with that, how to be friends with someone that she was so attracted to but who was so hung up on someone who'd passed away. And who could blame him? It had only been a few months. The best thing she could do would probably be to leave Drew alone.

But she couldn't stop being aware of him as he moved around behind the bar. When she'd entered the shop, he'd been chatting with an older gentleman. He'd glanced up at her, but by the time, she'd waited through two customer's coffee orders, he'd ducked through the kitchen door and left another barista to take her order.

Maybe it was just a coincidence. He was at work. She couldn't expect him to cater only to her if there was work to be done.

She hoped that was all it was. Hoped they could still be friends. She could temper her expectations—what expectations? She knew he was leaving in a few weeks. They could remain friends.

She glanced at her watch one more time. Daniel was a half hour late for the date. That was as good as three strikes in her book.

She stood to leave.

She'd been so caught up in her thoughts of Drew that she hadn't noticed what was going on outside the windows. On the sidewalk, a camera crew with three cameramen and a fourth guy holding a boom mike, was headed toward the door of the coffee shop. A moment later, they bustled inside, following a guy about her age.

One camera remained on the guy they were obviously taping, and two others panned the interior of the shop. Behind the boom mike guy, a woman entered wearing a headset and carrying a clipboard.

What was this, a reality show? In Ross,

Oklahoma? They had to be kidding.

To her horror, Mr. Reality TV star looked around the room until his gaze settled on her.

"Oh no," she whispered. She looked around frantically for a place to hide, but there wasn't even an emergency exit she could duck through without passing the cameras.

Mr. Reality TV approached, a fake, smarmy smile spreading across his face. "Angie? You look just like your picture."

Two of the cameras swung her direction, and a bright light had her squinting.

She held both hands in front of her face. "I don't want to be on camera."

There was enough space between her fingers for Angela to see the lady with the clipboard. "Cut! We'll start back outside again."

The camera guys lowered their devices and started backing away.

"Aw, Angie," Daniel whined, "what was that?"

"My name is Angela," she said, lowering her hands. "And what exactly was *that*?" She waved at the people trooping out the door.

The woman with the clipboard hustled her way up to the two of them. "Hi, there! I'm Juliet." She stuck out her hand, but Angela just stared at her. Seriously?

She pinched herself, but she didn't wake up from this nightmare.

"So we were hoping for a really great, authentic first-time meeting with you, but that's okay! Give me five minutes to get the cameras set up again, and we'll do a second take. You'll need to act surprised, as if you haven't met Daniel before—"

Angela was already shaking her head. "I don't want to be filmed, and I don't give my consent for you to use what you already taped."

"Aw, babe—chill out."

She really wanted to slap the man standing next to her. She turned her glare on him instead. "I don't appreciate being ambushed like this. I could've saved you a lot of trouble if I'd known you were going to try to film our date. I'm not interested."

He opened his mouth to protest, but a familiar presence stood behind Angela.

"This is private property, and your crew can't be in here."

She sent Drew a grateful look. He sent her the slightest wink and crossed his arms. "You're messing with our patrons who just want to drink their coffee in peace."

Most of the people in the shop were watching avidly and appeared to be eavesdropping on the entire thing. She was never going to live this down.

The wanna-be TV star and his producer

apparently weren't going to give up that easily. Daniel started arguing with Drew.

Drew leaned down to her. "Why don't you go hide out in the kitchen?"

She shot him another grateful look and crept away, aware of all the eyes on her as she slipped behind the counter.

Daniel was still talking.

"Do you want me to call the cops?" Drew interrupted him. "Because I will."

She ducked through the kitchen door and let it swing closed behind her, muffling the conversation happening in the front.

She leaned against the door, trying to catch her breath. What the heck had just happened?

She was still near-hyperventilating when someone pushed the door behind her, bumping her into stepping forward.

"Sorry." It was Drew.

"It's your kitchen. Well, sort of your kitchen since it's Wes's kitchen—"

She was so shaken that she would've kept rambling if he hadn't pulled her into his arms.

He held her loosely, his shoulders broad enough for her to hold onto. His breath ruffled the fine hairs at her temple.

All the tension she'd held onto suddenly burst free. She started laughing, at first giggles bubbling from her lips and then all-out belly laughs. She had to let go of him when she bent in half, laughter shaking her shoulders and sending tears streaming down her cheeks.

Finally she straightened, wiping her eyes with the sleeves of her shirt pulled over her fists. Oh, that had helped.

"They're gone," he said oh so helpfully.

"Good." And that sent her into a mini fit of giggles all over again.

She pressed both hands to her face. "I cannot *believe* that happened! Here in Ross, of all places."

"Yeah, it definitely seems like something that would've happened back in NYC. Not here."

Her face felt flushed when she finally met his eyes. "I don't know what I'm doing wrong. Maybe it's something I've written on my profile. Or the way I wrote it. I seem to be attracting the worst of the worst."

He smiled, one corner of his mouth ticking up. "Somehow, I doubt it's your fault that that guy decided to show up with TV cameras."

She shook her head at the absurdity of it.

"Thanks for letting me hide in here." She glanced around. She'd been in the coffee shop hundreds of times, but she'd never been back here. Along one side of the long room were shelves neatly organized with supplies, paper mugs and sleeves and lids and sugar packets. Along the other wall, a counter led up to an industrial stove and microwave.

"No problem. How's my cooking buddy?"

"Still raving about your spaghetti and meatballs. He's at his grandma's for the weekend. I had a couple of major baking jobs, and she loves to have him spend the night."

"I see."

It was awful, but that awareness bloomed between them again. She felt it, almost tangible in the air.

She glanced away, not wanting to make him feel awkward.

Her phone buzzed in her pocket. *Heard what happened at coffee shop*, the text message from her friend Jo read. Then a second quickly followed the first. *Sorry u struck out again. Hope he doesn't stake out your house.*

Angela grimaced. Her three friends were obsessing over her dating adventures. Somehow she'd become the guinea pig who got to go first on the whole dating game, but the time would come for Jo and Morgan. Mary Beth already had a serious boyfriend. They'd all four been a part of the pact, even if her friends weren't actively participating now.

"What's the matter?" Drew asked.

"Oh, a friend just texted. I'm pretty sure she was joking, but she told me to be careful if Mr. Reality TV stakes out my house."

Drew's face darkened. "You didn't give him your address, did you? Or post it on your profile?"

She sent him a withering look. "I'm not that stupid. But Ross is a small town. He can look in the phone book and find me."

"You should crash somewhere else for the night, then."

"I can't. I have baking to do. It's highly unlikely that he'd do that, anyway. He's probably halfway back to the city by now."

He untied his apron, then tugged it over his head, revealing the plain black T-shirt underneath and making her too aware of his muscled physique. "You're not going home alone."

Well, that was macho, and uncalled for. She tried to make a joke out of it. "You telling me you're a security guard in your regular life?"

He didn't crack a smile. "Nope. Not a cop, either."

"This isn't New York," she said. "If he shows up again, I'll call my friend's uncle down at the police department."

He shook his head. "I'm not negotiating on this. He got pretty mad there at the end when I wouldn't let him back here to talk to you. So you're not going home alone."

"I can't ask—"

"You can repay me in cookies."

Now it was her turn to cross her arms. "Why should I repay you when you're inviting yourself over? Making something out of nothing? Besides, I don't have time to babysit you. I really have to work. It's going to take me hours to frost this cake, then I have to deliver it."

He shrugged, keys jingling in his hand as he motioned her toward the back door, the opposite direction from where she'd parked. "Fine. I'll take you home and sit in my car outside your house."

Stubborn man. She pinched the bridge of her nose, trying to find another solution to keep him out of her space. Not that she minded, not really. It was a friendly, if unnecessary thing to do.

She couldn't think of anything, and he was staring expectantly at her as he held the door open for her.

Which was how she found herself half an hour later with a mountain of a man sitting on one of her kitchen barstools, watching her roll out white fondant on the counter.

CHAPTER SIX

The 4 things your friends say you are...
ToastedDuck: "Class clown. Courageous hero. Lifelong student. Mama's boy."

Cassandra, one of the college-aged baristas at Wes's shop, had been quick to tell Drew that he'd missed Angela while he'd been on his supper break. It seemed like everyone was interested in his—nonexistent—love life. Ever since last weekend when he'd helped her cart the three-tiered wedding cake from her house to the church, it seemed as if all eyes had been on him. Them.

It was annoying. He'd forgotten about this facet of small town life. Now that he was under the microscope, he'd never forget it again.

Had she been on another of her dates tonight? The last one had been disastrous. At least she'd been able to laugh about it. Jennifer would have freaked out for days, but not Angela. She'd laughed away her tension and then seemed to forget about the whole thing in a flurry of work.

He'd been amazed at her skill as she'd put the cake together. He and Jennifer had baked a cake together once when they'd first been married. They'd used butter knifes to load on frosting from a canister and made a huge mess of it—and each other.

Angela's cake was nothing like that. He'd seen a cooking show or two and knew what fondant was, but it seemed so much more finicky as Angela worked with it. Then she'd created a multitude of tiny flowers, some with fondant, some with colorful icing. She'd been rubbing her wrist by the time a few hours had passed and the cake was covered on one side with a cascade of flowers.

They'd kept up a running conversation the whole time. She'd told him about her childhood in Ross and the ten-year reunion she and her friends were planning, about Thad's birth and early childhood and some of his antics. She'd even opened up and told him a little about her divorce. He'd seen how her ex-husband had hurt her, even though she hadn't come out and said it.

She'd been very open with him. He hadn't reciprocated. There'd been one opening in the conversation where it would've been natural to talk about Jennifer, but the words wouldn't come.

The natural lull in the conversation had turned into an awkward silence until she'd filled it with details about the wedding she was baking for.

They'd texted a couple of times since the weekend, just casual notes, keeping things safely in the friend zone.

He hoped her date tonight would appreciate her. Her independent spirit that had prompted her to open her own business. Her obvious love for her son. The joy that shone from inside her.

He finished his shift and let Wes take over as evening was falling. Couldn't get his mind off of Angela's date, wondering how it had gone. As he got into his car, he briefly thought about texting her. That wouldn't be too creepy, would it? Just friendly?

He was driving by the bigger park across town when he spotted her car parked near the softball fields. He didn't think about it, just pulled in to a spot nearby.

It was sultry and humid—Indian summer in full bloom—as he stood next to his car, scanning the park for her. Looked like a church league softball game was in full swing on the ball field. The stadium lights had just kicked on.

He spotted Angela's bright copper hair at a picnic table that overlooked the field. She was surrounded by guys. They appeared to be most of a recreational team and wore sweaty jerseys and dirt-streaked baseball pants.

Was one of them her date?

Drew was halfway across the parking lot before he thought better of interrupting her. Last thing she needed was him stalking her or ruining her date. He couldn't help but wonder if she was having fun.

He paused behind a crowd watching the game. Her back was to him where she was sitting on a picnic table with her feet on the bench seat. One guy was perched next to her with a bottled water in one hand, but he was in deep conversation with the guy on his other side. He gestured out to the field and kept yakking. Was that the date? Lame. He was completely ignoring Angela.

Drew watched another few minutes, and the lamebrain was still ignoring her, so Drew got out his phone and typed out a text.

You look bored.

She pulled her phone out of her pocket. Her head darted one way and then another. Finally, she looked over her shoulder.

He gave a slow wave. She smiled and even in the semi-darkness, he saw the white flash of her teeth. His gut kicked.

He typed out another text.

You need a rescue?

Desperately.

I've got an emergency, he typed this time. He

didn't feel guilty about the fib at all.

He saw her jump up off the table, surprising the guy next to her into noticing her presence. She gestured animatedly, then jogged toward him.

Her hair was up in a cute ponytail, and her khaki shorts showed just enough of her shapely legs to draw his attention. He forced his gaze up to her tank top, which wasn't better. It might have been keeping her cool in the warm evening air, but had him a little warm under the collar.

"Thank you," she said as she came close. "I had no idea that a date could turn into a guys' night out with all his friends. He didn't seem that into me."

Guy was obviously an idiot. "No sweat." He started toward his car, happy when she followed him.

"So what's the emergency?" she asked with a wry smile.

He held the door open for her. "I've got a really bad craving for Chinese takeout."

She shook her head. "There's not a Chinese place in Ross."

He knew that. Ross was so small that only a limited number of restaurants could survive.

"I know. That's the emergency. We should pick up Thad and drive to OKC and find one."

It was silly to drive two hours just for takeout, but the idea had come to him, and when she lit up, he knew it was brilliant.

She sent him a sideways glance over the roof of his car. "So you moonlight as a taxi driver?"

He just shook his head and got in.

Thad jumped in the car at the babysitter's house, radiating heat and happiness and smelling like only a little boy at the end of a summer night could.

"Buckle up," he and Angela said at the same time.

"Jinx," she said quickly with an ornery grin. "You owe me a Coke."

He responded with a smile even as his heart panged. Jennifer had loved goofy jokes and silly pranks.

He worked to refocus his thoughts as he turned onto the two-lane road that would dump them on the highway in a few miles.

"How's it been going, man?" he asked Thad. "You been treating your mom right?"

In the rearview mirror, he saw Thad nod earnestly. "We made cookies for my teacher's birthday."

"That sounds like fun." It sounded like something he would've liked to do with them.

They found a hole-in-the-wall place open late, and Angela disappeared to use the restroom.

Apparently the place only served take-out, because there was only one table for two against the far wall. Drew and Thad stood together several feet out from the counter, staring at the menu board.

"What do you like?" Drew asked, setting his hand on Thad's shoulder. He did it without thinking, but the natural movement gave him a pang like he'd felt earlier. What would his and Jennifer's kids have been like?

Thad shrugged. "Dunno."

"You like spicy stuff?"

Thad shook his head.

"Okay, so the spicy Kung Pao chicken is out."

They discussed other possibilities. Then Thad looked up at him, and it was clear by the way his eyes had dimmed that he had more on his mind than sesame chicken. "The other day you told me it was okay to cry. But what do I do if those two guys try to beat me up again?"

Drew had expected the question when he'd babysat the other night, but it had never come up.

Now, he let his hand rest on Thad's shoulder again. "If there's an adult around, ask for help. If there isn't and you're alone with those guys, there's no shame in running. Two against one isn't very fair."

He squeezed the boy's shoulder gently. "What you really need is a pack of friends. I had Wes when we were young, we stuck like glue to each other until college."

Thad looked down at his shoes. "That's kinda hard because Jack moved away. And I'm not very good at making friends."

The last was said in an almost-whisper.

Drew propped his hands on his knees and got down on the boy's level. "I think you're an awesome guy. You've got mad baseball skills and a great dog. And your rock collection and everything you know about them is really interesting."

Thad looked up at him with a sideways glance. "Rocks are kinda dorky."

"Says who?"

Thad shrugged. He still looked so dejected.

Angela approached, the click of her shoes on the linoleum floor alerting the guys to her presence.

"Tell you what. Wes said the last superhero night at the coffee shop was a huge success. And he's doing another one." Drew looked up at Angela to bring her into the conversation. "If you can convince your mom to bring you, I can make sure there are some other guys your age there, and you can meet them."

Angela shot him a questioning glance even as Thad looked up at her with a pleading glance.

"Can we go, Mom? Please?"

Drew mouthed, *I'll tell you later.*

She shrugged. "I don't see why not."

Great, she'd agreed. Now Drew needed to find some kids to come.

CHAPTER SEVEN

How do you typically spend your leisure time?
Maximus884: "I love to read. Academic journals, mostly."

Somehow, Angela had ended up at superhero night again. At least this time her date wasn't barely old enough to be legal or wearing a costume.

Nope. This one was wearing a tweed jacket with leather patches on the elbows. She'd once seen a picture of her father in his early twenties with the same jacket on. She couldn't stop thinking about that. The man's glasses kept slipping down his nose, and he kept pushing them up, over and over again.

Over her date's shoulder she could see Thad spinning on one of the barstools, Drew leaning on his elbows behind the counter talking to him.

She'd had so much fun with Drew and Thad the night they'd gone for Chinese food. They'd laughed a lot as they'd gobbled down Chinese food sitting on the curb in the parking lot of the takeout restaurant.

Then she and Drew had conversed in softer tones on the drive home as Thad drifted off in the backseat.

He'd finally copped to his profession, an investment banker.

He was a suit, which had surprised her, disappointed her. She'd promised herself not to fall for someone who had a high-stress job that required long hours. She'd been there with her ex-husband, and she didn't intend to go back.

But Drew had confessed that his wife's death had made him rethink a lot of things—like the long hours spent in his office. And she couldn't help but wonder if she'd judged all men in corporate jobs too harshly, as if they were all just like her ex.

And then after she'd lugged a sleeping Thad up to his room and put him to bed, she and Drew had sat for a long time on the hood of his car. He'd told her the entire conversation he and Thad had at the Chinese place. She'd been near tears thinking her son didn't believe he could make friends. But Drew had offered to set up a sort of low-stress play date during the superhero night for Thad and some other kids that had come in last time.

She trusted him to watch over Thad while she was on her date.

She might trust him too much. She certainly liked him too much. The impromptu Chinese food road trip was the best date than she'd had in a long time. And she'd had a lot. And that was dangerous, because she knew Drew was headed back to New York in another month.

She was determined to have a good date tonight. This was number seven in a line of pretty awful ones, and surely, surely this time would be better.

"So tell me about your career," she said, leaning slightly forward, letting her focus slide off Thad and Drew and onto the man in front of her.

"My official title is Urban Entomologist. I'm an adjunct professor at State University right down the turnpike, but my real passion is a project I've been working on for a couple of years with the state park over in Oak Lakes."

She felt like she should know what an entomologist was, but she was a little fuzzy on the particulars. "Oh. What does your project entail?"

"I'm doing a long term study of the different insect populations. Last year there was a bagworm infestation, and the year before that we had a whole colony of Elm Leaf Beetles."

An involuntary shiver went down her back. "Oh. Wow."

He went on to tell her about the fascinating mating rituals of a certain type of dragonfly, but before he could go into why older houses in Oklahoma—like hers—were a breeding ground for Brown Recluse Spiders, she pushed her chair back from the table.

"I'm so sorry, but I don't think this was the best idea."

His shoulders slumped. "Too much?"

She nodded vigorously.

He sighed. "My last date said the same thing. It's just...you're so pretty, and I get nervous around beautiful women. And insects are my passion—"

"Thank you for meeting me," she said quickly. Maybe it was cruel, but there was absolutely *no* future for them.

She made her way to the counter, keeping tabs on the entomologist with a glance over her shoulder. He was already threading his way through the crowd of superheroes toward the exit.

Thad had disappeared, but Drew greeted her with a smile at the counter. She sidled up and turned to show her back to him, craning her neck to see over her shoulder. "Do you see anything crawling on me?"

"No, why?"

She shook her head as she turned to face him. She still had the heebie-jeebies and barely resisted the urge for a full body shake. Her scalp itched, and she scratched it, threading her fingers into her hair. Bugs. Why did it have to be bugs?

"Where's Thad?" she asked. Maybe she could distract herself from the feeling of minuscule feet crawling up her spine.

Drew nodded to the back corner near the restrooms. There were four boys, including Thad, all huddled around a low table, heads bent over something spread across the table.

"He's showing the other boys his superhero comic collection."

Her brows drew together. "He doesn't have a comic collection."

"He does now."

Her heart felt like the Grinch's, growing bigger until it threatened to burst. "You didn't have to do that."

He focused on scrubbing a patch of the countertop with his washrag. She could see his cheeks turning red. "It wasn't a big deal. They were just taking up space in a box in my mom's attic."

And he'd taken the time to find them—probably a more monumental task than he was admitting to—and given them to Thad. If they were from his childhood, they might even be valuable.

"It's a big deal to Thad." If it made a way for him to make friends with more boys his age, it was a *huge* deal. Her voice was slightly choked as she said, "And it's a big deal to me."

Drew's eyes lifted, and their gazes connected. She swallowed but didn't look away. She knew he didn't want the connection between them, and she didn't blame him. He was still grieving his wife. So she was trying to keep things friendly, but her feeling were venturing dangerously into non-friend territory.

Wes came up behind Drew and slapped his shoulder. "That's my brother, altruistic to a fault." Wes winked at her. "I keep telling him to be a little more selfish."

This was said with a pointed sideways glance at his twin, one that Angela couldn't decipher but that had Drew shoving his brother's hand away.

Wes reached back and slung his arm around Drew's shoulders. Drew wrestled back, finally shoving his brother.

"Live dangerously," Wes called out. "And take a break."

Drew shook his head as he untied his apron.

"What was that about?" she asked.

Drew shook his head again. He tilted his head toward Thad. "I think he'll be okay for a few minutes, don't you? Wes'll watch out for him. Wanna sneak outside with me?"

She did. When he motioned her forward, she followed him behind the counter, through the kitchen, and out the back door. There was a small row of parking spots, and then the curb turned to a small grassy area with a park bench beneath an old oak. She sat beside Drew on the bench.

He pulled her up onto the top of it, their feet on the bench, their shoulders almost brushing.

"I can't thank you enough for helping Thad." She tilted her head back and looked up through the tree's branches. One or two twinkling stars were visible through the nearly bare canopy. "Sometimes I wonder if it was the right thing, letting Thad's father go. He wasn't invested in us, but maybe I could've worked harder."

Drew nudged her with his elbow. "I know you. You didn't give up without a fight, did you?"

She bit her lip. Thought about what she hadn't in a while. "I did try my best. For Thad and for our family. But it wasn't enough. Maybe I wasn't enough."

Drew jumped off the bench, whirling to point a finger at her. "Don't you dare think that. I've only known you a short time, but everything I've seen is...well, you're beautiful, inside and out."

She climbed off the bench and marched toward him. "It's all fine to say that, but what about these awful dates I've had? If I'm as desirable as you say I am, why can't I find a decent guy?"

He ran a hand back through his hair. "I don't know what those dudes' problems are. If they can't see what's right in front of them—"

He cut himself off, staring down at her where she stood, right in front of him. She nearly smiled at the irony.

He seemed to be wrestling with himself. She didn't dare breathe.

And then he reached for her. It seemed the most natural thing to do to come into his arms. His head bent, and his lips captured hers in a searing, melting kiss.

She felt the chaos of his emotions, the grip of his hands at her waist. She held his shoulders tightly, returning his kiss, willing him to know that she felt this crazy connection too, that she wouldn't hurt him, not for anything.

And then his kiss, his touch turned tender. One of his hands came up to thread through the hair at her nape. His mouth brushed hers once, twice more.

And then he pulled away. He shoved both hands into his hair. "I shouldn't have...we shouldn't have..."

She reached for him. "It's all right—"

"It's not all right! Not for me." He jerked away

before she could touch him, spinning wildly toward the shop's back door. She thought he'd stalk away, but he turned to face her again. "I'm sorry. I..."

She had never wanted this for him, the crashing grief that he couldn't even seem to contain. "*I'm* sorry."

He shook his head. "I'm going to tell Wes I'm taking off."

"I'll get Thad."

He was already striding away before she'd finished, yanking open the door so hard it crashed against the brick wall.

She took a breath, then another, trying to calm her rioting emotions. Rationally, she knew she hadn't done anything wrong. Maybe she should've stayed inside, shouldn't have come out here with him at all, but he'd asked, and she'd wanted nothing more than to be with him.

She wished fervently that she'd had a connection with one of her disaster dates. Someone available. Someone who could love her and wasn't leaving forever. Someone who wasn't Drew.

She hadn't meant to fall for him.

Now what was she going to do?

CHAPTER EIGHT

What does your ideal Saturday morning look like?
Love2Bike: "Coffee, the newspaper, and a lazy morning."

Drew was hiding in the coffee shop kitchen.

There was no other way to describe it. He was a coward. All because Angela was out there with a date again.

A week had passed since they'd kissed. Since *he'd* kissed *her.* It had definitely been him who started it, though she'd been a more than willing participant.

He'd forgotten about everything in those moments. Until reality had intruded. Until he'd seen the image of his wife. He'd betrayed Jennifer.

He'd slammed his way back inside and told Wes he was leaving. He'd meant it, disappearing into the woods with a tent and a small backpack for three days before he'd come back home, looking and smelling like a grizzly bear with a temper to match.

He hated himself for not feeling more guilt over what had happened. Hated that his feelings were so mixed up.

His phone rang, startling him from where he stood propped against the prep counter.

Wes.

He cleared his throat and swiped the call to connect. "Yeah?"

"Just calling to make sure you're still at the shop."

Wes's tone was short. His brother hadn't been happy with Drew's disappearance, since he'd had to find a last-minute replacement for two missed shifts at the shop.

"I'm here," Drew said through clenched teeth.

"You sound tense. Is Angela up there?"

It would've been polite of her to find another venue for her dates. Even though the Cup of Joe was the only place in town for a coffee date. He couldn't fault her. He was the one flashing mixed signals, going hot and cold. She'd been nothing but sweet.

He was the one who was messed up.

"You gonna forgive yourself for whatever happened Saturday night?"

No.

"Why not?"

He hadn't meant to say that aloud.

"Leave it alone, Wes."

"You're my brother. When you bleed, I bleed."

He should have just hung up.

For some reason, he left the line open.

"No one's judging you. No one thinks it's too soon except you, man."

He sniffed loudly. He wasn't tearing up, just had a burning behind his nose.

"Are you going to stay single forever? Would Jennifer have wanted that?"

She hadn't. She'd told him so. But he'd never expected to have feelings for someone so soon.

Wes rang off after reminding him not to walk out of the shop. Drew wouldn't be that irresponsible, even if he didn't particularly want to face Angela right now.

She was still there when he emerged from the kitchen fifteen minutes later. Based on the way she leaned forward in her chair, legs crossed toward the good-looking guy, she seemed to be having a good date.

They were still there when he started rounding up stranded coffee cups and later when he wiped down the counter. The place emptied, and then it was ten minutes past closing time.

Angela and her date were in their own little world.

The searing knife in his gut was jealousy, plain

and simple.

He cleared his throat, and when that didn't work, called out, "Hey, guys, I'm closing up."

They looked up, surprise in their expressions as they realized everyone was gone. Angela looked at him, and he saw the curiosity and compassion in her eyes.

"Sorry," the guy said as they stood.

Angela didn't say anything as they left, the dude holding open the door for her.

And the knife in Drew's gut turned.

Through the window he watched them stop between their cars to continue their conversation. He twirled the lock violently.

He went through the motions of cleaning the machines and checking the till for tomorrow's starting cash, adding up the bank deposit—he had to recount twice because his concentration was shot—then locking the back door before he hauled two huge garbage bags to the Dumpster around the side of the building.

He dumped the trash, then glanced at Angela's car.

Dude was gone, but Angela remained. She was seated in the driver's seat with the door open.

The very last thing he should do was walk over there, but his feet carried him that way before he could talk himself out of it.

She had her phone out, head down, screen lit.

Maybe texting someone. His gut felt on fire wondering if she was already texting the guy who'd just left.

"That seemed like what a date should be," he said.

Her head came up. "Hi."

"I wasn't sure if you were still talking to me."

Her head tilted slightly. "After you ran to hide in the kitchen, I thought it might be better if I kept my distance."

She was obviously smarter than he was.

"Did you like that guy?"

Her eyes went unfocused as she contemplated his question. "It turns out we went to rival high schools. Mostly we were talking about mutual friends."

Mostly wasn't everything. His gut churned.

"Are you jealous?" she asked.

Only an idiot would admit it, but, "Yeah. I shouldn't be, but I am." He shook his head. "It's not fair to you, because I can't give you any hope."

Even from two yards away, even with the height difference of him standing and her remaining in the low car, he could see the hurt in the depths of her eyes.

He didn't want to be the cause of that. "It's not you—"

"You don't have to offer me cliches." She

shook her head and looked down at her lap." I get it."

He ran both hands through his hair, grabbing and pulling it away from his scalp. "I wish I did."

She fiddled with her keys, and he was afraid she was going to go. He didn't want her to. "Wes thinks I'm being absurd," he blurted. "He doesn't see any issue with me being attracted to you." It was so much more than that, but he couldn't say it aloud. *The heart wants what the heart wants*, his brother had said more than once.

She looked back up at him, her eyes squinting slightly. "If you ever wanted to talk about her, I'd be happy to listen. No strings. No expectations."

He didn't know if he could do that. But he wanted to give Angela something, and maybe this was it.

"We met at my high school graduation. She was a year older than me and attending for a friend."

She'd been so gorgeous in a peach-colored knee-length dress that flared when she walked. He'd gotten tongue-tied and flustered but had managed to ask for her number.

"I'd been planning to go to school in Texas, but she was at school in Philly, and all of a sudden, I changed my plans. My parents wanted to kill me, but one of my scholarships was transferable, so I went. I didn't know anybody in

Pennsylvania but Jennifer. We were engaged a year later."

Those days were both shining and hard. Working and taking a full load at the same time. Spending every moment they could together. It hadn't been enough.

"After we got married, we lived in this tiny apartment—so small we couldn't both be in the kitchen at the same time. We'd fight, and there was nowhere for me to go to release my temper—so we learned to talk through it. Not that we fought all that often."

It got hard to continue, and he swallowed hard, looking down Main Street, where all the businesses had closed down for the night.

"What was she like?" Angela whispered.

"She was this...free spirit. One Thanksgiving, we couldn't afford to come home to Oklahoma, so she invited everyone on the same floor of our apartment over to share a meal. We had so many people packed in our place."

He laughed a little at the memory. "She was quiet. Soft-spoken. But she had this wicked, sarcastic sense of humor, too. She loved living in the city."

He missed her with such ferocity.

"How did she die?"

"She got this really rare form of cancer. No one in her family had even had a brush with cancer before. She fought hard, but..."

It had been a long battle. Almost four years. Ups and downs and times when he felt sure she'd make it through. She hadn't. He'd fought with God for a long time, even before she'd passed. He still didn't have peace about it. Why take someone so young, so vital?

He'd needed her.

"I'm sorry," Angela said. "So very, very sorry."

Tears burned his throat. "She was supposed to live this long life. I mean, I had plans for our fiftieth anniversary party, you know? Now..." He was lost. All those plans, all the expectations for their life together. He was adrift.

He expected more questions from Angela. *Don't you ever want to remarry? When do you think your grief will ebb?*

But she didn't say anything. She just sat in her car, breathing with him as his chest clutched and released, until he evened out and could breathe again.

Angela was special. He knew it. It wasn't going to be long before one of these dodos she was dating figured it out and snatched her up.

He couldn't breathe again thinking about that. The sense of grief at the thought of losing Angela was almost as potent as what he felt for Jennifer.

But that couldn't be right. He'd loved Jennifer. He didn't—

He hadn't—

He couldn't have fallen in love with Angela.

The heart wants what the heart wants.

He backed away, fear choking his throat. "I have to go."

He was half afraid she could see the realization of his feelings in his expression. And then what?

Because nothing had changed for him, not really.

CHAPTER NINE

What are your three best life skills?
ChadRBurger: "Playing guitar, original pickup lines, and kissing."

The shop was half empty as Angela sat across from Brian again. She'd had a good time with him a week ago and agreed to a second coffee date.

But it was the man behind the counter that had her attention and probably always would.

She loved Drew. She hadn't meant to fall for him, but it had happened anyway.

She'd realized it last weekend. He had a deep capacity for love. He'd shown it in his actions toward Thad, helping her son overcome his nervousness and fears about making friends. And she'd heard it in his voice as he'd spoken about his wife. They'd had something special, maybe something a person only found once in a lifetime.

And it was obvious he wasn't going to find the

same with Angela. He might be attracted to her, might like her, but it hurt him too much to be with her.

And he was leaving.

She hadn't been enough to keep Rob's love. Hadn't been enough to make him stay. Why did she think she would be enough for someone like Drew, who already had a life far away?

So she kept smiling at Brian, kept laughing at his description of one of his high school basketball coaches whom she remembered seeing at away games. He was nice enough, even if he didn't make her heart leap. Maybe she'd set her sights too high, wanted passion when she was only good enough for mundane. Mundane was easy. Mundane didn't hurt.

"Wanna go get some real food?" Brian asked. "The cafe down the street doesn't close for another couple hours."

That sounded better than sitting here all too aware of Drew behind the counter.

"Sure. Let me go freshen up."

As she passed, she kept her eyes averted from Drew, who was in a quiet conversation with his brother behind the counter.

She made a quick stop in the restroom, then washed up. She hadn't slept well the last few nights and looked it.

She splashed her face with water, then patted

dry with a paper towel.

It didn't help. Maybe because the exhaustion she felt was more than skin deep.

She reapplied her lipstick. She could try to look good, even if she didn't feel it.

She took a deep breath before she pushed out of the small room. And emerged into chaos.

Brian and Drew were both standing, in each other's faces. Brian said something she couldn't hear.

And then Drew shoved Brian, shouted right in his face.

"Stop!" she cried.

The tussle continued as Brian shoved back, and a chair was knocked over. The table she and Brian had been sitting at was already on the floor, the remains of her coffee spilled across the tile in a brown mess.

She darted forward, ready to slug someone herself, but Wes blocked her way and held her there. "Why don't you stop them?"

Wes didn't answer, and she struggled to get away when she saw Brian throw a punch.

Drew ducked out of the way. Brian wasn't so lucky as he caught an elbow with his nose and mouth.

"Stop!" she cried again.

With one last shove, Drew pushed Brian several steps back, though Brian remained on his feet.

"Get out," Drew growled.

"Drew!"

He glanced at her, ran an agitated hand through his hair.

She moved toward Brian. What had provoked the fight?

"You can't go with him," Drew said.

And that put her hackles up. "You can't tell me—"

"He spiked your drink!" Drew burst out. "I don't know what he put in there, but—"

"I did not."

Wes, still with his arm holding her in place, looked at her. "I saw it, too." He turned to Brian. "I'm calling the cops." He let her go, but there was no reason to keep holding on to her now. She felt frozen in place.

Brian's eyes darted to her, but this time she read the guilt on his face, the slump of his shoulders. She turned away, turned her back to both him and Drew, her chest suddenly banded tight.

She clutched both her elbows, arms crossed over her middle, as fear and hurt crashed over her. She started shaking.

The chime over the door rang. Probably Brian was leaving. Hopefully he was never coming back.

"You wanna sit down?" Wes was back and he drew her away from the center of the shop to a more secluded corner, though she felt the eyes of other patrons following her every move. "Sheila's calling the cops for me."

Most of the folks in town had been quietly curious about her dating habits, watching but not commenting, which she was thankful for. But this...when word got out that she'd almost been the victim of a date rape drug or whatever it had been, what would they think? Would her reputation suffer? What if word got back to Rob and he tried for full custody, claiming she was a bad mother?

This whole thing had been a mistake. She should never have made that pact with Jo, Morgan, and Mary Beth.

The whirlwind of emotions caught up with her. The events of just now plus everything that had happened with Drew. She cried, covering her face with both hands to hide her tears, as if they didn't all already know.

She turned to face the wall and wrapped her arms around her middle to try to hold in the sobs. She could leave. She should leave, but she didn't know if she could see past her tears to get to her car.

"I f-felt like I knew him," she mumbled through her tears. "We had some of the same friends back in high school."

Wes patted her shoulder. "This isn't your fault."

How could it not be? She'd been the one to accept his online friendship, accept a second date.

She was aware of Drew's presence, could feel him hovering nearby.

"I just f-feel so stupid." Why couldn't the good guys, the *guy* she wanted, return her feelings?

Wes murmured something she couldn't make out above the sound of her own sniffles.

He moved away, and then Drew was there, gently touching her hunched shoulder. "Angela..."

She couldn't stand it.

"No!" She pushed out of the seat, whirled on him. She pointed a shaking finger at him. "You don't get to do this. You can't pick and choose when you want to be a part of my life. "

"I know." Drew's hair was mussed, and one cheek had a small scrape across it. She'd never seen him so disheveled, and his eyes reflected a matching chaos.

Wes shifted from foot to foot, anxiously watching them.

"Why don't you guys go somewhere more private and talk?"

She shook her head. "I don't think it's a good idea for us to go anywhere together."

Drew shoved his hands in his pockets.

"You made me care about you." She pointed her finger at him. Her hand was still shaking. "I know you didn't make any promises, but I started having feelings for you anyway."

"I never meant to hurt you." Of course he hadn't meant it, but that didn't change anything. It didn't change her heart.

She couldn't absolve him of his guilt even if she wanted to.

"I'm leaving town," he said.

"I know."

"Soon," he said. "Not like I originally planned. I'm leaving in a couple days."

She knew it was for the best, but it still hurt to hear.

She wrapped her arms around her middle, trying to hold herself together. She bit her lip, and then shored up what courage she had left.

"I'm going home now."

But home was no better. Her house was empty. Thad gone to play at one of his new friend's houses for the evening and wouldn't be back until later.

She had a cake order for next week, but she couldn't work on it yet. Without her son in the house, with no distraction from her thoughts, everything was too painful. She broke down in tears.

Why couldn't she be enough? What was so wrong with her that she couldn't find a man to stick?

CHAPTER TEN

Which family member are you closest to?
ChefEric: "My sister. I'm twenty-six, and she still bosses me around."

Angela would've given up on the online dating altogether if not for her three friends and the pact they'd made. When she showed up for her next online date at the coffee shop, one week later, Drew was nowhere to be seen.

CHAPTER ELEVEN

It took a month.

Drew went back to his job, back to the small one-bedroom apartment he'd shared with Jennifer. He ate at their usual haunts, places he hadn't been able to visit since she'd died.

But nothing went back to normal. Wes checked on him twice a week, though his brother was careful not to mention Angela or Thad.

It didn't keep Drew from thinking about them.

Fine. He'd fallen in love with her. And his feelings about it had begun to change, maybe before he'd even left Ross. When he'd seen that creep spike her drink, he'd gone a little crazy. In the split second he'd imagined what could have happened to her, he'd gone berserk. He'd wanted to pummel the man, and it had been good to have Wes at his back. He'd barely controlled himself.

That's when he'd known his feelings were more than just caring about Angela. That's when he knew he'd fallen in love with her.

The night she'd asked him to talk to her about Jennifer had softened his grief somehow. Talking about and remembering the very things he'd loved about his wife had brought the good times to the forefront of his memories. Those long, aching days at the end had been hard, filled with grief even before Jennifer had passed. And it had stuck with him.

Until he'd met Angela and her crazy dating antics had cemented her place in his heart.

The question was, what was he going to do about it?

"I thought I'd find you here."

He looked up at the female voice. Brittany. Jennifer's younger sister.

"What are you doing here?" He hopped off the bench overlooking Central Park, one of his and Jennifer's favorite places to sneak off to on the weekends. They loved to people watch, loved guessing where the tourists came from.

Jennifer's little sister lived in New Jersey, and he hadn't seen her since the funeral. He shared a friendly hug with her.

"Wes called me."

"He did?" Drew hadn't known his brother even had Brittany's phone number.

"He said something about you falling in love with a gal back in Oklahoma."

Heat flushed his face, but he didn't look down. His feelings were so muddled. Should he feel ashamed?

Brittany sat on the bench and he joined her there. Looking out over the water, it was a little easier to say, "Yeah, I did."

She was the first person he'd admitted it to, and saying it aloud released something in him, like helium leaving a balloon.

"What's her name?"

"Angela. She has a seven-year-old son." He couldn't help smiling a little as he said it.

They stared at the water for several moments. "If you think the family would judge you for marrying again, we won't."

He shook his head slightly. "It isn't that... I just... At first, it felt like I was betraying Jennifer to have feelings for someone else."

"At first?"

He squeezed the back of his neck. "I dunno. I—lately, I've been rethinking everything."

She touched his hand. "Jennifer's gone," she whispered, and her eyes were wet. "No matter how much we wish she weren't, she's gone. And if you fell in love, then I say, good for you."

Her words were freeing, an echo of what he'd begun feeling since he'd left Ross.

The question was, what should he do about it?

~ * ~

It took him another week to make it back to Ross.

It was lunchtime when he hit town. He didn't go to Wes's house or the coffee shop. He went straight to Angela's place.

She and Thad were playing in the front yard. It was still fairly warm, and it looked like she'd been gardening. Now she was chasing her son around the leaf-strewn yard with a hose. Water squirted in swirling arcs, droplets spraying every which way. Thad shrieked with laughter. Halloween decorations spilled out of two boxes sitting in the open garage doorway.

Drew pulled up to the curb, parked the car, and got out. He leaned one elbow on the top of the car as he stood inside the open door. Just watching, letting his heart fill up at seeing them again.

Thad saw him first. "Drew!" The boy darted in his direction, and Angela's water spray followed.

"Hey!" Drew ducked, letting the spray fall on his back. It stopped quickly.

He straightened in time to step around the door and catch Thad in a fierce hug when the boy vaulted toward him.

"Mom said you had to go home," Thad said,

looking up at Drew but still holding on.

Drew ruffled Thad's hair, letting the boy scoot back. "I'm back now."

"Thad," Angela called from the middle of the lawn.

The boy started back and looked over his shoulder to make sure Drew was following. He was, even if the back and shoulders of his shirt were a little damp.

"Hey," he greeted her as his feet hit the lawn.

But she looked more wary than welcoming.

His heart thumped hard against his sternum. Was he too late?

She'd turned off the water from the spigot and now held out the dripping end of the hose to her son. "Please wind up the hose and then go into the house."

"Aw, Mom." Thad looked over his shoulder again, and Drew winked at the boy. Thad smiled a little and went to do as she'd said, though Drew noticed he was moving as slowly as molasses and kept sneaking glances their way.

Angela didn't say anything until he was close to the corner of the house, almost out of earshot. "What are you doing here?" She crossed her arms. Not exactly the welcome he'd hoped for, but that was his own fault.

"I'm here to ask you out on a date."

Her eyes widened infinitesimally, but other

than that, her expression remained neutral.

"Isn't that a long way to travel just to ask someone out on a date?"

He grinned. "Not if you're in love."

Her arms dropped, and he could read the naked hope on her face. But he wasn't done yet.

"I wasn't sure the best way to get this to you, so I printed it out." He held out a single sheet of white paper and was gratified when she accepted it. She started reading.

He already knew what it said. He'd written it.

Username: Not2Late

What are your three best life skills? Driving in bad traffic, being a shoulder to cry on, making a mean espresso.

How do you typically spend your leisure time? I sometimes get too caught up in work. Looking for someone to challenge me on this. Playing catch could be a start. Maybe helping with homework?

Other than appearance, what is the first thing people notice about you? My temper.

Things I'm looking for in a woman: Someone with a kind heart, someone who loves her son, someone who is patient with me when I'm being stupid.

Interests: Bakers, golden retrievers, rock collecting, and reading comics.

What I hope to get out of this date: Spending time with the woman I can't live without.

He watched her eyes scan back and forth

across the page. It went on front and back. When she finished and her gaze rose to him, she was biting her lower lip. Her eyes were a little moist.

"Do you really mean it?" she whispered.

"With all my heart."

He reached for her and she came into his arms, settling there like she belonged.

"I love you," he murmured into her temple.

She gave a little half-sob. "I love you, too."

He squeezed her waist, emotion filling his throat in a hot knot.

"But I thought—"

"You thought I was going to be stupid forever," he said.

She pressed a kiss into his shoulder. "What changed?"

Everything. "Nothing changed in the way I felt about you. I started falling for you from the beginning. As to how I feel about Jennifer—I think I'll probably always love her, always miss her. But she's not here, and I don't want to miss out on living the rest of my life."

And he wanted Angela and Thad to be part of it.

He touched her cheek.

She leaned up on her tiptoes to meet his kiss, and he obliged her. This kiss was even better than their first, a tender promise for today and all their tomorrows.

When Thad ran back around the side of the house, shouting enthusiastically, they broke apart. Drew chuckled.

She brushed her hair behind her ears.

Thad ran around them in circles, talking so fast Drew couldn't understand half the words.

"I guess we should talk logistics," she said softly.

He raised his brows in question.

"With us here and you in New York..." she prompted.

"I'm not going back to New York," he said. "I already packed up my apartment. It's all in a truck somewhere in Ohio right about now."

Her eyes filled, her smile tremulous. "Really?"

"It's time for a fresh start. In a lot of ways. For now, Wes is taking me on as a partner. In the future...? Who knows. I might even learn how to bake."

She held up the printed paper he'd given her, now slightly crumpled from her grip. "I might decide to frame this."

"As long as you close down your online profile, you can do whatever you want with it. No more superheroes or bug dudes for you."

She laughed. "Agreed."

"Drew, can you play catch with me?" Thad said. "Can you stay for dinner? Are you gonna marry my mom?"

He laughed, joy pulsing through him so fast, it felt like it was emerging from every pore.

He held Angela's gaze. "Yeah, buddy, I'll play catch with you. And I'll stay for dinner, if your mom wants to cook. Or we can crash over at Wes's place if she doesn't."

He held a pause, sensing the boy was listening hard but still not daring to look away from Angela.

"And yeah. Not today, but soon, I'd like to marry your mom."

"Whoohoo!" Thad's shout rang out in the neighborhood, but Drew had pulled Angela in close again and was only half paying attention as the boy made wild war shouts and danced across the yard.

Drew was all wrapped up in her, and he couldn't be happier about it.

"I love you," he whispered as their foreheads touched. "To heaven and back."

"Me too."

He didn't know what he'd done to deserve two happy endings in his life, but he wasn't going to complain.

He'd never have guessed that online dating would bring Angela into the coffee shop—and into his life. All it had taken was ten dates.

ABOUT THE AUTHOR

USA Today bestselling author Lacy Williams works in a hostile environment (read: four kids age 6 and under). In spite of this, she has somehow managed to be a hybrid author since 2011, publishing 32 books & novellas. Lacy's books have finaled in the *RT Book Reviews* Reviewers' Choice Awards (2012, 2013, & 2014), the Golden Quill and the Booksellers Best Award. She is a member of American Christian Fiction Writers, Romance Writers of America, ALLi, and Novelists Inc.

Made in the USA
Lexington, KY
27 February 2017